Ophelia Martin Spofford

A Norse Romance

Ophelia Martin Spofford

A Norse Romance

ISBN/EAN: 9783337347833

Printed in Europe, USA, Canada, Australia, Japan

Cover: Foto ©Andreas Hilbeck / pixelio.de

More available books at **www.hansebooks.com**

A

NORSE ROMANCE

BY

MRS. O. M. SPOFFORD

G. P. PUTNAM'S SONS
NEW YORK   LONDON
27 WEST TWENTY-THIRD STREET   24 BEDFORD STREET, STRAND
The Knickerbocker Press
1892

A Norse Romance

by

Mrs. W. M. Spofford

Dedicated
to my Son
WILL.

The Siren sang in her ocean cave,
  Weaving her spells the while -
Amber and pearls with gifts of the wave,
  Laced she with charm and guile.

For far, far away dwelt a
              maiden fair,
        And as the wild rose sweet
For her was wrought the jeweled
              snare
        That sought her dainty feet;
    Yet still the song rose soft and
              clear,
        Above the summer sea -
    With swell and sigh, now far,
              now near,
        It fell enchantingly.

Oh come my love and float with me
Along the silvery waves,
Oh come my love and dance with me
Within the coral caves

There knelt to sue by the maiden's side
An earl of high degree

And soon he'd bear his lovely bride,
   Across the throbbing sea —
For this lover true was a Viking bold,
   Who ruled o'er sea and land —
And well the story of love he told,
   As he prayed for her snowy hand.
Oh! could they but hear the festal lay,
   As borne on the breeze's wing;

Like song of birds
at close of day
When in leafy cells
they sing.

"Oh come my love and float with me
Along the silvery waves,
Oh come my love and dance with me
Within the coral caves."

The sea-king stands near his prow of gold,
Ruling his argosy -

The warlike chant of his sailors bold
    Rings out stern and free.
A hundred spears are flaming bright,
    A hundred shields as suns;
The crimson banner flaunts in light,
The Dragon homeward turns.

A liquid voice as a vesper peal
Thrills through the ambient air-
Its charms upon the senses steal,
Its odors sweet and rare-
Oh come my love and float with me
Along the silvery waves-
Oh come my love and dance with me
Within the coral caves."

The siren calls to her ancient gnomes,
Come, tritons strong as well.

They sing in throngs from their ocean homes,
At sound of the nereaid's shell -

The ladies team all with haste prepare
A cavern dark and deep.

Where all alone with dread despair,
  The Norseman's bride shall weep.
For like the wind-harp's softest notes
  Across the shimmering sea –
Sweetly the song around them floats
  That mystic melody:

„Oh come my love and float with me
  Along the silvery waves.
Oh come my love and dance with me
  Within the coral caves."

Like winged masts the waves rise,
Or sink with sullen roar.
From deep green depths the lurid eyes
Of monsters seem to lower.

But the war-ship speeds upon her flight
Arched with mist and spray,

Till in the noon-day's saffron light
Her oars fresh in the bay!

No more they hear the witch notes borne,
  Across the swelling main—
But he whose deck is but a throne,
  Takes up the sweet refrain:

Oh come my love and dance with me
While music softly falls—
Oh come my love and dwell with me
Within my bannered halls